It was a very person
and it was Irene, in f
blood. Letting Andre
harmlessly by, she le
next firmly past Rak
the timbers of the ch

'One-nil to Irene, I think,' Duggie mocked
from a safe distance.

Andrew was not amused . . .

Andrew Weston is furious when the
headmaster invites *girls* to join in cricket
practice – and even more furious when
Irene Day is picked for the school team.

But Irene has some big surprises in store
for Andrew and his brother Chris. And
when their team looks in danger of defeat
at the hands of Manor House School's star
batsman, only a very special player can
save the day . . .

Rob Childs is a Leicestershire teacher
with many years experience of coaching
and organizing school and area
representative sports teams. He is the
author of three previous sporting tales
about the two Weston brothers, THE BIG
MATCH, THE BIG RACE and THE BIG
DAY, all published by Young Corgi Books.

Also by Rob Childs,
and published by Young Corgi Books

THE BIG MATCH
THE BIG RACE
THE BIG DAY

THE BIG HIT is one of a series of books,
BY MYSELF books, which are specially
selected to be suitable for beginner
readers.

THE BIG HIT

ROB CHILDS

Illustrated by Tim Marwood

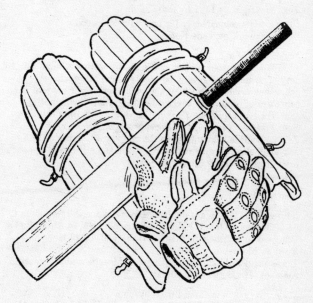

YOUNG CORGI BOOKS

For all young cricketers,
boys and girls –
keep playing and enjoying the game!

THE BIG HIT

A YOUNG CORGI BOOK 0 552 52662 2

Originally published in Great Britain by Young Corgi Books

PRINTING HISTORY
Young Corgi edition published 1991

This book is set in 14/18pt Century Schoolbook by
Kestrel Data, Exeter

Young Corgi Books are published by Transworld Publishers Ltd,
61-63 Uxbridge Road, Ealing, London W5 5SA, in Australia by
Transworld Publishers (Australia) Pty Ltd, 15-23 Helles
Avenue, Moorebank, NSW 2170, and in New Zealand by
Transworld Publishers (NZ) Ltd, Cnr Moselle and Waipareira
Avenues, Henderson, Auckland.

Made and printed in Great Britain by
The Guernsey Press Co. Ltd, Guernsey, Channel Islands.

1 Over and Out

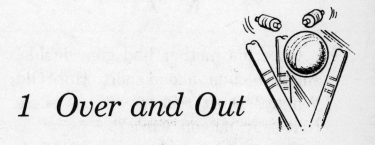

'*Owzat!*'

Andrew Weston's shriek of delight echoed around the garden, bringing his mother to the back door.

'Andrew, please!' she called, a little crossly. 'Don't make so much noise.'

'Sorry, Mum,' he said, not really meaning it as he gloated over the wreckage of his younger brother's wicket.

'Think of the neighbours. You'll frighten the life out of poor Mrs Witchell, if you're not careful.'

Once his mother had gone inside, Andrew let out a loud snort. 'Huh! Old Witchy? Don't reckon witches scare that easy, do you, Chris?'

'What? Oh, doubt it,' said Chris vaguely, his mind more on wickets than witches, wondering why he'd been clean bowled yet again. 'Probably got nine lives, anyway, like that scraggy black cat of hers.'

Andrew grunted in agreement. 'Bet she's got at least nine of our tennis balls as well, seeing as she never lets us have any of 'em back when they go over the wall.'

'You mean when *you* belt them over,' Chris said. 'It's not me.'

'Only 'cos you can't. Not against a

brill fast bowler like me,' Andrew boasted. 'Just look at that mess. Stumps all over the place.'

'OK, OK, don't rub it in, I can see.'

'You didn't see the ball though, did you?' he smirked. 'Go and fetch it, it's my turn to bat again.'

Chris groaned. If anything, his bowling was even worse than his batting, and he didn't hold out much hope of being able to join eleven-year-old Andrew in the Danebridge Primary School cricket team this year.

'C'mon,' came the shout. 'Give me one of those lovely, juicy, full tosses of yours so I can smash it out of sight.'

'Go easy, will you, this is our last ball.'

'Don't worry,' Andrew laughed. 'Grandad will get us some more. He always does.'

'Why should he?' said Chris. 'I don't think it's fair on Grandad, the way you lose them faster than he can buy them. Anyway, remember what he told you the other day.'

'What was that?'

'About you skying the ball far too often. Keep it down on the deck more, he said.'

The boys' grandad took every chance he could to watch them play their sports and was never slow to pass on a few tips. Now Andrew thought about it, he decided Grandad might perhaps have a point, bearing

8

in mind the number of times he'd been out, caught, last season.

'OK, I'll give it a try for a while,' he sighed, 'but it sounds a pretty boring way to bat, if you ask me.'

Normally Andrew didn't take much notice of all the boxes and buckets spread around the lawn as pretend fielders. He loved to thump the ball right over the top of them or, even better, to blast it straight back past Chris into the vegetable plot. But now he forced himself instead to steer each shot more accurately through the various gaps until he could stand it no longer. Unfortunately, however, Andrew's patience ran out at exactly the wrong moment.

He lashed out just as Grandad showed up to join in their game and, as soon as he hit it, he knew it was too close to the bowler. If there was one thing Andrew openly admitted that his kid brother *did* do well, both in cricket and when playing in goal, it was catching a ball. So he wasn't a bit surprised when Chris suddenly hurled himself to his left and snatched the ball out of the air with one hand.

'Fine catch, Chris,' Grandad praised him, and then gave his usual little chuckle. 'But next time, try and get two hands to it!'

Chris grinned and claimed the bat back in triumph, guessing Andrew would serve up an extra-fast delivery straightaway in order to seek his revenge. He was right, too. But it was also a wild one, well wide of the wicket, and Chris slogged at it hopefully, never dreaming he'd actually succeed in making contact.

Whack! The ball soared up and away, clipped the top of the wall and spun off towards disaster. 'Oh, no!' he wailed helplessly.

CRASH!

'Crikey, now you've gone and done it!' cried Andrew.

Chris panicked and fled, pausing in mid-flight only to jam the bat into his brother's hands as he tore headlong for the gate. 'Here, it's your bat, you have it.'

'I don't want it. Come back!' Andrew yelped. 'Hey! Wait for me.'

Grandad was still gaping dumbly at the damage, pipe drooping from his mouth, when he found himself suddenly lumbered with the weapon.

'Sorry, Grandad, all yours,' gasped Andrew, making his own rapid exit. 'Got to go. Bye!'

It was a double disappearing act faster than any witch could have achieved. By the time Mrs Witchell peered from her upstairs window to see the smashed windowpane of her greenhouse, and their mum arrived in the garden to find out what had happened, the boys had vanished.

The two women slowly switched their attention from the broken glass towards the tell-tale bat, dangling suspiciously at Grandad's side.

'Oh, Dad! How could you?' accused his daughter. 'You're worse than the kids sometimes, you really are.'

2 Rivals

'Girls!' Andrew scoffed. 'They wouldn't dare – would they, Duggie?'

His pal, John Duggan, shook his head. 'Nah! They'd better not, anyway. Let them stick to their own little games.'

Mr Jones had them worried. When they read the headmaster's notice saying that girls were welcome to join in the cricket practices this term, they thought he was kidding until Tim Lawrence put them right.

'I shouldn't count on it, if I were you,' the school soccer captain said. 'There was a girl in the team a couple of years ago when I first got picked.'

Andrew was shocked. 'What! Actually playing for the school?'

'Yep, she was pretty good, too,' Tim nodded, before teasing them even more by calling to a group of girls across the corridor. 'Any of you lot there thinking of doing cricket?'

'Belt up, you idiot,' Duggie hissed, but it was too late.

Irene Day had broken away from the others to come and look at the notice. 'Hmm, why not?' she said. 'Might be good for a laugh.'

Andrew snorted. 'This is cricket,

not some kind of soppy joke.'

'Sounds funny to me, listening to my dad,' she replied. 'The way he goes on about bowlers having square legs and short legs and things.'

Her friends giggled, making Andrew see red. 'They're just names of fielding positions, stupid. Like fine leg and silly mid-off.'

This only made them laugh even more. He gave up and stormed off outside, barging into anyone who was unwise enough to get in his way.

'Oh well, that settles it,' Irene grinned. 'If it annoys Andrew so much, I'll definitely play. Let me borrow your pen, Tim, and I'll write my name on this notice right next to his.'

Andrew's worst fears were confirmed when the cricketers set off to walk down to the village recreation ground for their first practice session.

There were three girls amongst them, but what really made his eyes pop was seeing Irene in a proper white cricket sweater. Like most of the others, Andrew didn't yet own such a thing himself. And she even had the nerve to be carrying a brand-new bat!

He deliberately drew level with her as they crossed the footbridge over the narrow River Dane which skirted the recky. 'Where did you get those from?' he demanded.

'What?' she asked, knowing exactly what he meant.

'Don't act daft,' he snarled. 'The bat and the jumper.'

'Oh, them! Dad went out and bought them for me straightaway when he heard I was taking up cricket. He's dead pleased.'

'Huh! Takes more than fancy gear to make a *girl* into a cricketer.'

'Ah, pleased to see you two getting on so well already,' Mr Jones interrupted, taking no notice of the boy's protests. 'Pad up, both of you, and you can bat together.'

Andrew reddened with embarrassment. 'Bet old Jonesy has done that on purpose, just so I can't bowl a few fast ones at you myself,' he muttered in disgust.

Irene shrugged. 'Yes, pity! I was rather hoping I might take *your* wicket today as well.'

'Huh! No chance!' he retorted. 'That'll be the day, when a girl gets Andrew Weston out.'

'I'll look forward to it then,' she said cheekily.

Buckling her pads on swiftly to make sure she reached the pitch ahead of him, Irene chose the batting end before Andrew realized what she'd done. 'Hey! I'm facing first,' he cried.

'Doesn't look like it,' she answered, calmly taking up her position. 'Have to be a bit quicker next time, won't you?'

Unexpectedly, Andrew suddenly burst out laughing and pointed at her. 'Look, lads, she doesn't even know the right way round to stand!'

'I'm left-handed,' Irene said simply, making him feel foolish as everyone loudly jeered his mistake.

And it soon became obvious, even to Andrew, that she knew perfectly well how to handle a bat, too, stroking the second ball she received towards the wooden changing hut for four runs.

Putting the girl in her place was not going to be as easy as Andrew had thought, but he was determined to get his own back. After blazing a couple of shots away himself, he pushed a ball straight towards where Duggie was fielding and then charged down the wicket, calling late for a run.

Startled, not expecting a quick single, Irene hesitated, but again Andrew screamed at her. 'Yes! C'mon, run!'

He was nearly up to her by now and reluctantly she set off. It was suicidal. Duggie didn't even have to throw the ball to run her out. Laughing, he sprinted to the wicket with it in his hand to knock off the bails before Irene could reach the crease.

Andrew found it difficult to stop grinning as well until the headmaster turned on him. 'You're out instead, young man. And for trying to pull a mean, selfish trick like that, you have now lost any chance you might have had of being named captain!'

That was a bitter blow for Andrew and he spent the rest of the practice in a deep sulk, aiming any further taunts only at his brother's efforts. Especially when Chris later became Irene's first victim.

'Fancy being bowled by a girl!' he shouted as Chris trailed sadly away, knowing Andrew would not allow him to live it down.

But help was at hand. Grandad's stone cottage backed right on to the recky and he had been watching the practice from his garden wall with great interest. Like Mr Jones, he was impressed with the girl's steady, accurate left-arm bowling and called Chris over to him.

'Never mind, you won't be the last boy that blonde lass baffles this year,' he sympathized, then asked, 'Who's the little lad you were batting with? I've not seen him before.'

'Rakesh Patel. He's new,' Chris said. 'Says he bowls spinners, too, so he'll probably get in the team. Guess I won't, though.'

'You might do yet,' Grandad

encouraged him. 'I've been thinking. Why don't you ask your Mr Jones if you can have a go with the gloves?'

'Wicketkeeper, you mean?'

Grandad nodded. 'Aye, why not? You're a good fielder and I reckon you could be even better behind the stumps, the way you love diving about in goal. Ever tried it?'

Chris shook his head. 'At least it might get me out of having to bowl, I suppose.'

It proved to be the turning point for Chris. Once he'd been allowed to put on the big padded wicketkeeping gloves, he never looked back. They felt a bit stiff and strange at first, of course, but he soon got used to them

24

and let very little slip past him. And when Mr Jones threw him the gloves at the start of the next practice, his hopes rose.

Another promising performance from the youngster convinced the headmaster that he had found his school team's wicketkeeper, and Chris was thrilled to be chosen for the first friendly match at Shenby. He raced over to swamp Grandad with the news, Andrew following more slowly, brooding.

'Oh dear, Andrew. Why so glum?' Grandad asked.

Chris, still bubbling, got in first. 'It's because Tim's captain, and not him.'

'No, it's not,' Andrew scowled. 'It's

that Irene. Jonesy's gone and picked *her* as well! Shenby will think we're a bunch of sissies, turning up with a girl in the team.'

'Don't be so silly, Andrew,' Grandad told him off. 'Why shouldn't she play, if she's worth her place?'

'Well . . . well . . .' Andrew stumbled. 'It's a boys' game, ain't it? It's not meant for girls.'

'What nonsense! Lots of girls and women play cricket,' Grandad said. 'Anyway, admit it, she's a good all-rounder.'

'She's not bad . . .' Andrew gave way slightly, before adding with a sneer, 'for a girl, that is, of course.'

3 Catches Win Matches

'I've won the toss and put them in to bat,' Tim Lawrence told his team. 'Then we'll know how many runs we need to get.'

Andrew disagreed. 'I'd have batted first, if it'd been me. Knock up a big score ourselves and let them do the chasing.'

'It's *not* you though, is it?' Tim smiled, suspecting that Andrew's bad mood over Irene and the captaincy hadn't exactly been improved by getting out of the school minibus to find

a girl cricketer in Shenby's side too. 'Anyway, cheer up, I'm relying on you to skittle them out.'

When the girl herself came out to open the Shenby innings, Andrew began the match by bowling at his very fastest – and wildest. His first effort flew so wide that neither she nor Chris behind the wicket had any chance of reaching it and the ball scorched down to the boundary.

'Four wides,' called Mr Jones, one of the umpires, stretching out his arms as a signal to everyone. 'Steady up, Andrew, and go easy on your brother. He's bound to be feeling a bit nervous.'

Andrew wasn't really bothered

about any problems Chris might be having and pounded in again to launch another rocket. The ball zoomed past the opener, beating her all ends up for pace, but just shaved the stumps. It also went straight through Chris for two extra runs.

The young keeper looked down at his gloves, half expecting to find a hole in them somewhere. It was perhaps just as well for him that he didn't

glance up towards where Andrew stood in the middle of the pitch, hands on hips, fuming like a smoky chimney.

Fired up properly now, the bowler's next three fierce deliveries all had the girl and Chris hopping about, neither quite sure which side of the wicket the ball would fizz by. Chris did very well to block them, in fact, but the last ball of the over was snicked wide and low to his right. He dived, got a glove underneath it and then had the ball jerked out of his grasp as his elbow hit the ground.

Andrew had already whirled round to scream for the catch, but Mr Jones shook his head. 'Not out – I'm afraid he's dropped it.'

Andrew was furious. 'What a wally!' he shouted at his brother.

'Hold your tongue, Andrew,' the headmaster ordered. 'You won't bowl again in this game for language like that on the cricket field.'

Nor did he, and without Andrew, Danebridge's bowling attack looked to have about as much bite as a new-born baby. To add to his misery, Irene claimed two of the wickets that eventually fell, but their hopes of winning were not helped by several more missed catches.

In the end, it was Rakesh they had to thank for keeping Shenby's final score down to sixty-nine runs. His slow, skilful bowling bagged him four

wickets, one of them shared with Chris – the highlight of the innings as far as Grandad was concerned. The spinner tempted the batsman into leaving his crease to try and wallop a high looping ball, but he was fooled by its flight, missed it completely and Chris wasted no time in stumping him.

When Danebridge batted, however, they found Shenby's fielding on top form. Both the openers, Tim and Duggie, went cheaply to brilliant catches and six wickets were down when Irene walked in to join Andrew. Immediately it was seven as she lost her middle stump, first ball.

'Quack! Quack! The golden girl gets

a golden duck!' he sniggered, and there was little Irene could do in response except stick her tongue out at him as she left.

But the score itself was no laughing matter. Danebridge had only twenty-three runs to their credit and were staring at a heavy defeat when Rakesh came trotting in to bat.

'C'mon, Andrew, we need some of your big hits,' he said. 'I'll give you as much of the strike as I can.'

That was the kind of thing Andrew liked to hear. But he was soon gasping for breath as Rakesh showed what a fast runner he could be between the wickets.

'Hey! Slow down a bit,' Andrew

panted, leaning on his bat and grinning. 'I will have to smack a few biggies now to save my legs.'

He started straightaway, clubbing the bowler for two fours in a row, and when, in the next over, he was lobbed the kind of ball that just sat up and begged to be clobbered, Andrew granted its wish. With a huge heave, he pulled it powerfully away for six, clearing the boundary flags by a mile.

But as the ball began to fall, Grandad clapped his hands over his face, not wanting to look. 'Oh no! Not my lovely car, please . . .'

His faithful old motor was parked next to the school minibus, right in the path of the dropping bullet. He heard

the crash of broken glass and children's cheers, but when he finally peeked between his fingers there didn't appear to be a mark on it. He could hardly believe his eyes.

It was only after Grandad saw the headmaster himself running towards the vehicles that he noticed the smashed side window of the minibus.

Mr Jones groaned as he inspected the damage. 'If I didn't know any better,' he sighed, 'I'd swear Andrew might have done that on purpose.'

Success went to Andrew's head. When he tried to repeat the stroke, his luck ran out and he miscued. The ball was sliced high into the air and a fielder waited confidently for it to come swirling down out of the clouds.

'Mine!' he shouted and hugged the ball safely to his chest, making a very difficult catch look almost easy.

Andrew had notched up twenty-eight, his highest-ever score, but it wasn't quite enough to give his side victory. Despite Rakesh's best efforts, and even five scrambled runs from Chris, Danebridge still finished three short of their target.

Mr Jones gathered the whole team together before they left for home. 'Never mind about the result,' he told them. 'You've learnt a good lesson here today about a wise old saying in cricket . . .'

He winked at Grandad who guessed what was coming.

'Catches win matches!'

4 Bat and Bowl

The cricket ball thudded cleanly into Chris's gloves once more and Grandad rubbed his aching shoulder with a certain satisfaction.

'Well taken,' he called out, 'but my poor old bones are telling me that's enough for one day. Let's go and join the others.'

Helping Mr Jones give the squad extra fielding practice, Grandad had been throwing the ball at the wicket-keeper non-stop for the past fifteen minutes. He'd made Chris run and fetch it whenever he missed one, but he reckoned his arm was far more tired than the boy's legs.

The headmaster decided to call a halt as well, pleased with the way everyone had worked hard to improve their skills. He had some good news for them as a reward. 'Manor House, the big private boys' school, is celebrating its centenary this year,' he announced, 'and they've invited us to take part in a special cricket tournament there.'

'Centenary?' Andrew asked. 'What's that?'

Grandad answered, wincing at a sudden twinge, 'It's a bit like being

one hundred not out, which is about as old as I feel at the moment.'

Mr Jones laughed. 'Never mind, it's all in a good cause. I'm sure we shall enjoy a great day out. Shenby will be one of the four teams involved too, plus Selworth.'

'Selworth!' Rakesh piped up. 'Wicked! That's my old school.'

'Yes, but the snag is, I'm afraid, that I can't pick many of you. It's only a six-a-side tournament.'

Rakesh need not have spent the night worrying. When the cricketers rushed to the sports noticeboard the next morning, his name was there among the chosen six, along with Tim's as captain. So, to their relief, were those of Andrew and Duggie, but it didn't take them long to go on to the attack.

'What's *she* doing there?' Andrew demanded, pointing to Irene Day's name on the list. 'Those boys from Manor House will have a fit when they see her turn up. I bet they don't even know girls exist!'

'Lucky things!' cried Duggie. 'I wonder what they're going to make of a bowler wearing a skirt?'

Andrew giggled. 'Well perhaps, with a bit of luck, they'll be laughing so much they won't be able to bat properly!'

As for Chris, he didn't mind if Irene bowled in a leotard and green wellies.

He was just happy to see he'd kept his place as the team wicketkeeper.

Twenty runs came off Duggie's loose over, as Tim and Irene made the most of the wide open spaces between fielders in their practice match for the Sixes.

'Sorry!' he grinned sheepishly at Andrew. 'You know I'm not the best bowler in the world.'

'You're not kidding. You're not even the best bowler on Danebridge recky. But I am – as *she's* now going to find out.'

This was the first real chance Andrew had had to bowl at Irene and he couldn't wait to show her who was the boss. But it was a moment she had been looking forward to as well. In her own quieter way, she was just as determined to come out on top.

It was a very personal head-to-head duel, and it was Irene, in fact, who drew first blood. Letting Andrew's opening ball zip harmlessly by, she leaned back to cut his next firmly past Rakesh to rattle against the timbers of the changing hut.

'One-nil to Irene, I think,' Duggie mocked from a safe distance.

Andrew was not amused, and as Irene tapped him away for a single to lose the strike to Tim for the rest of the over, it wasn't until his second go later on that he gained a bit of

revenge. By then, however, she had already scored nineteen runs and was only out because of taking a wild swipe at a straight ball, eagerly looking for more.

'Bowled you!' Andrew cried for effect, but everyone knew it no longer mattered. The damage had been done and Tim's team were well on the way to an easy victory. Even Chris's duck made no difference to the final result.

Neither did Andrew's. And what made it even harder for him to take, was that his kid brother joined forces with Irene to dismiss him.

Andrew had found her slanting left-arm bowling very difficult to deal with, and when a slightly wider delivery came along, he flung his bat at it in frustration. Unfortunately, the ball bounced up more than expected and he edged it through to the keeper.

'Owzat!' Chris chorused gleefully with the bowler to appeal for the catch.

Andrew flared up. 'You could have dropped it. Whose side are you on, anyway?'

'Tim's at the moment,' Chris grinned back. 'And you're out!'

'Quack! Quack!' Irene mimicked him as he stomped off, prodding viciously at the pitch with his bat as he went. 'This must be that day we talked about when a girl gets Andrew Weston out.'

'Hit a bad bump,' he muttered as an excuse. 'That's what did it.'

'No, you're just a poor loser, that's all,' she replied.

It was Grandad who came to Chris's rescue after the game. 'Forget about it, Andrew, and come over to the cottage. I've got a surprise for you both.'

There, laid out on the large kitchen table, were two full sets of cricket clothing – boots, white flannels,

shirts, sweaters, the lot.

'Wow! Are they for us?' gasped Andrew in disbelief.

'Well, they won't fit me,' Grandad chuckled. 'I can't have my grandsons turning up at a posh school like Manor House on Saturday in any old gear.'

The brothers raced to see who could get into their kit first. 'Fantastic, Grandad, thanks,' came a muffled voice from under a sweater, which he took to belong to Chris. 'Now I feel like a real cricketer.'

'You look like one, too,' Grandad replied when Chris's head reappeared. 'If you look smart, you play smart, that's what I always say.'

'That's right!' said Andrew, posing in front of the hallway mirror and playing an imaginary shot. 'You're magic, Grandad. Thanks! Wait till Irene gets an eyeful of these.'

'Pals again?' Chris asked, hopefully.

Andrew grinned. 'Sure thing, little brother. Sorry about some of the things I've said. I get kinda carried away sometimes playing cricket. So watch out now, everybody! Here come the Westons in white . . .'

5 *Hit for Six*

Mr Jones wisely parked the minibus in front of the school building, well out of range of any cricket balls.

As the Danebridge players noisily spilled out on to the crunchy gravel, they were met by a well-spoken boy in a striped blue blazer. 'Welcome to Manor House,' he began. 'I'm Roderick Palmer-Tompkinson, head boy and cricket captain. Please come this way.'

He guided them behind the school, pointing out the two pitches on the

large playing fields that had been specially prepared for the Sixes.

'What's the big tent thing for?' Andrew asked him.

'That is the marquee where we shall be treating you all to lunch,' Roderick answered politely, but Irene saw him eyeing her doubtfully up and down, kitted out as she was in white skirt and sweater.

'Don't worry about me,' she said,

slipping a wink across at Rakesh. 'I'm only here for the tennis!'

She practised an overhead serve, which only confused and embarrassed the boy even more, but Andrew was quick to step in. 'Take no notice of her, Rodders, it's just the way she bowls,' he joked, and was unable to resist having another dig at Irene directly. 'Bit different to the recky, eh? Nice *flat* wickets here.'

'Not still going on about that, are you?' she said, stifling a yawn before whisking off to greet the Shenby girl she'd spotted near the marquee. Rakesh, meanwhile, was enjoying a lively reunion of his own.

'Wicked!' he cried when the

Selworth captain told him they were meeting in the morning game. 'I'll grab a hat-trick against you with my deadly spinners.'

'What! Come off it,' one of his old mates laughed. 'Danebridge must be desperate if they've had to pick you and that girl.'

Rakesh grinned impishly. 'Ah, don't mock, she's our secret weapon.'

As it turned out, in fact, Irene remained a mystery to them. Selworth didn't see very much of her talents, either with bat or ball, but they still had no reason to laugh. Rakesh gave them far too much of a reminder, for their liking, of what *he* could do.

First, though, they had to suffer at

the hands of Tim and Duggie, who got their team away to a flying start. The two openers were still together after five overs, the halfway point of the innings, with the little scoreboard on the boundary already showing thirty-seven runs.

Andrew, due in next, was getting restless. 'C'mon, get out, one of you. I want my turn to slog it around.'

'Be patient,' Grandad said quite sharply. 'It's a team game, you know. You should be glad they're doing so well.'

Andrew pulled a bit of a face. 'Well, I am, but . . . I mean, they could bat all day against this lot. Even Chris could.'

'Oh, thanks a lot,' muttered Chris, adjusting his pads. 'I'm only wearing these ready for wicketkeeping. I hope I don't have to bat.'

'I hope you don't as well,' Andrew snorted. 'We would be in trouble if you had to go in.'

'Andrew!' The warning voice came again.

'OK, Grandad, sorry,' Andrew nodded. 'Team game, I'll remember.'

A loud appeal suddenly jolted him up on to his feet, hurriedly pulling on his batting gloves. 'Didn't see it. Who's gone?'

'Duggie,' said Chris. 'Out caught. Good luck.'

'No luck needed. Pure skill, little brother, just you watch.'

As ordered, Chris watched Andrew hit his first ball for four, and then watched him mishit his second straight back into the surprised bowler's hands. As for Andrew himself, he was so stunned to be out that he could only manage a sickly grin at Rakesh as their paths crossed on his slow trudge back to face the smirking Chris.

'Pure skill, big brother! I blinked and almost missed it.'

Andrew swallowed hard and coughed. 'Yeah, well, like Grandad said, team game, ain't it? Just doing Racky a favour. Thought it'd be a pity if he didn't get the chance to have a bash against all his pals.'

Chris stared, not knowing quite whether to believe him or not.

It was from that point onwards, however, that Rakesh began to take control of the game. He stayed with his captain to see the final score to seventy-two, thirty of them to Tim, a total that proved almost forty runs too many for Selworth. Although he didn't do the promised hat-trick, his clever spin bowling still claimed three wickets in one over, including two in two balls which both popped up for catches to the eager Andrew.

Along with Tim and Duggie, Andrew also collected one of the other wickets to fall and, in the end, he felt that the match had not worked out too badly – at least Irene had got no runs and no wickets.

'You needn't have bothered getting up this morning,' Andrew said to her as they left the field. 'We wouldn't have missed you.'

She shrugged. 'That's the way it goes sometimes. Perhaps it'll be my turn this afternoon.'

'Doubt it!' he scoffed and headed happily for the marquee. 'C'mon, gang. Time for lunch. Let's get there first before the other game finishes and have the pick of all the strawberries and ice-cream!'

Andrew was already helping himself to seconds by the time Danebridge

learnt that their opponents in the Final would be their hosts, Manor House. Shenby's keen fielding had not been quite enough this time to save them from defeat against the strong home team, and they now had to be content with a third place match against Selworth.

'Shame,' said Duggie. 'I was hoping to get even with Shenby.'

'Yeah, well, never mind,' Andrew replied through the smears of ice-cream around his mouth. 'That can wait. We'll just have to beat Manor House instead and spoil their hundredth birthday party for them.'

But Roderick Palmer-Tompkinson had other ideas about that, as Andrew was to find out to his cost straight after taking a wicket with the very first ball of the afternoon.

Having won the toss and elected to bat, Roderick was determined to enjoy himself. He arrived at the crease almost before the opener had left and immediately began to take Andrew's bowling apart, crashing him away for two boundaries on the trot, one of which sent the ball skimming through the open front of the marquee.

Andrew couldn't believe what was happening. 'OK, buster,' he snarled. 'Just you try that again.'

Roderick was not the kind of batsman ever to duck such a challenge. 'Righto, if you wish,' he said breezily.

Nor did he duck the next ball which whistled around his ears. He had half guessed what Andrew would do and was in position ready, swaying on to his back foot and keeping his eyes fixed on the speeding missile.

He whirled the bat round and hooked the ball high over the umpire's head for a glorious, thrilling six. It landed right in the middle of the neighbouring pitch like an unexploded bomb, scattering the startled players.

'Sorry, just not your day, it seems.' Roderick beamed at the dejected fast bowler.

Andrew was too shocked to reply. He'd never been hit for six before and now knew how other bowlers felt

when he did it to them. He also knew he had met his match.

'Whatever that kid might talk like,' he muttered to Tim before slinking off to lick his wounded pride, 'he sure ain't no wimp with the bat.'

Tim himself fared little better, giving away nine runs, and the scoreboard had rattled to twenty-three after only two overs. 'If Rodders can murder me and Andrew like this,' he shuddered, 'I hate to think what he's going to do to Duggie when he has to bowl!'

The captain tossed the ball to Irene. 'Your turn, and good luck,' he said, more in hope than expectation. 'If we don't get this guy out quickly, we've had it. He's going to win the match on his own.'

6 Six of the Best

'Well bowled!'

It was Roderick's habit to congratulate anybody who prevented him from scoring, but he rarely found himself having to repeat the praise in the same over. He realized now he'd just done so, and it bothered him – especially as this bowler was the girl who had teased him earlier about playing tennis.

When he missed her next ball as well, making three out of four he'd

failed to hit, the last of Irene's butterflies at having to bowl at the Manor House star batsman fluttered away. She floated in to deliver her fifth on a new bubble of confidence, and as Roderick stepped forward to try and drive the ball, it suddenly veered in towards him, beat his bat once again and rapped him on the pads.

'Well bowled,' he murmured, remembering his manners, and he meant it, too. He wasn't just being polite. No bowler had ever had him in such trouble. She was swinging the ball around so much, he didn't really know what to do about it, except pray he might survive the over.

Roderick wasn't the only one to be

having problems coming to terms with Irene's bowling. Andrew was also being forced to do some quick re-thinking about girl cricketers, amazed at how she'd got a stranglehold on the same boy who had hammered his own bowling all over the field.

Andrew watched as the worried batsman hesitated slightly before playing at the final ball, waiting to see which way it would move, but the split-second delay proved fatal. Too late Roderick jabbed his bat at it, only to chop it down on to his own stumps. He heard the dreaded crash of timber behind him and had no great wish to look back.

'Oh, well bowled!' he cried, despite

his disappointment, and as he strode off, Irene was mobbed in sheer relief by the rest of the team. Even Andrew was seen to pat her on the back.

'In the words of old Rodders, well bowled!' he laughed. 'I couldn't have done it better myself.'

'I know,' she smiled sweetly in reply.

It was the crucial breakthrough Danebridge had needed and, for a while at least, the tide turned in their favour. The scoring rate slowed down, and Andrew's second over saw the Weston brothers combining success-fully on the cricket field for the first time.

It was worth waiting for. The

batsman flicked at a ball from Andrew as it brushed past his legs and Chris took off, throwing himself to his left to grab it at full stretch in both gloves in spectacular style.

By the end of the innings, the Danebridge players had plenty of proof of their enthusiastic efforts in keeping the final total down to fifty-three. Although not all of them could match the outfits of the Manor House boys, there were grass stains on every item of white kit they wore where they had flung themselves to the ground to stop extra runs.

Andrew and Chris admired each other's evidence as they walked off, the keeper pointing out a long streak down his sweater. 'That's where I took that diving catch,' he said proudly.

'Brill! Look at these, too,' Andrew grinned, showing off his dirty flannels. 'Bet Mum's not going to be best pleased though, when she sees them in the wash basket!'

But if any of them thought the match was as good as won, they were soon made to think again. The Manor House bowlers were far better than Selworth's and made Tim and Duggie struggle for every run. The openers, in fact, could only scrape together seven runs off the first three overs and then both of them had their stumps flattened in the next.

Rakesh came and went too, caught

and bowled by Roderick for three, and at the halfway stage of their shattered innings, Andrew found himself batting with Irene with just sixteen runs on the scoreboard.

'The best form of defence is attack, that's what Grandad would say in a hopeless situation like this,' he told Irene between overs.

'Funny,' she smiled. 'That's just what my dad said to me a minute ago. So what about it, then?'

Andrew's face broke into a broad grin. 'OK, you're on. Let's give it a whack and see what happens.'

'Oh, there's just one thing,' she added as they parted.

'What's that?'

'Don't go hogging the bowling. I know which end to hold the bat.'

He nodded. After her bowling display against Roderick, Andrew was at last prepared to give Irene's abilities the respect they deserved.

Riding their luck at times, risking quickly-taken singles to give each other a fair share of the strike, their unlikely partnership took wing and they enjoyed a brave twenty-eight run stand. Both could easily have been run out or caught more than once but, as the scores grew ever closer, the fielders panicked under the pressure and fumbled their chances.

But it couldn't last. With her own score on twelve, Irene flashed her bat

at a ball, snicked it and the wicket-keeper gratefully held on to the catch.

'Great stuff, Irene!' Andrew called after her. 'Sorry you can't stay to finish the job off.'

'I'm sure you won't mind doing it for me,' she replied cheekily.

Chris joined his brother at forty-four for four with ten runs still needed and the final over of the match due to be bowled by Roderick himself.

'Don't worry if he gets you out – it won't matter,' Andrew told an anxious Chris. 'Last man stands, remember, in Sixes. They'd still have me to deal with.'

Roderick overheard. 'It will be a pleasure,' he said cheerfully.

'Don't count on it, Rodders,' Andrew

replied. 'I'm the one with the bat in my hand now, and I've still got a score to settle with you.'

But Andrew mishit his first ball, squirting it out in the wrong direction. 'C'mon, Chris, run! There's two there.'

They could only manage one. Chris stumbled and fell as he turned for the second, and Andrew had to slam the brakes on. He feared he might be the one run out, if they both finished up at the same end.

Roderick moved his fielders in close for Chris, but the ball clipped the edge of his wavering bat and skidded past the keeper for four runs. Without really knowing how, he had scored his first-ever boundary!

Chris relaxed a little. There were only five more wanted for victory, but any dreams he might have secretly held of socking a winning six himself were swiftly dashed. Next ball he was out, bowled, and all he could do now was to act as his brother's running partner.

'Bad luck, our kid, nice try,' smiled Andrew as they swapped ends, guessing what had probably crossed Chris's mind. 'But leave the biggies to me in future, OK?'

There were just three balls left for the match to be won or lost – and it was nearly lost by Andrew immediately. So determined was he to give Roderick a taste of his own medicine, that he charged right out of his crease to lash the first of these away but only swished at thin air. Fortunately for Danebridge, the Manor House wicketkeeper, in his haste, snatched at the ball and fluffed the stumping. The boy hung his head in despair, not daring to look up at his captain.

'Cool it, Andrew!' Chris warned him. 'Take your time and pick the right ball.'

Taking a deep breath, Andrew also took his younger brother's advice and played the fifth ball firmly but quietly back to the bowler. One ball to go, and Andrew concentrated hard, unaware of the silence that now lay over the

playing fields like a heavy blanket. Shenby had already won their match against Selworth and everyone was strung around the boundary edge, up on their feet and hushed, savouring the tense atmosphere of the final drama.

All that existed in Andrew's vision was the approaching bowler and then the shiny little red object whirling towards him. 'Here goes,' he decided. 'It's now or never.'

As it bounced, he took one giant stride forward and opened his shoulders, swinging the bat down like a golf club. The instant he made contact, he knew that he had never hit the ball so hard in his life. It went dead straight, high over the heads of the gaping Roderick and Mr Jones, the umpire.

All anybody could do, players and spectators alike, was to try and follow its path into orbit. It seemed to go higher and higher . . . well over the boundary flags for six . . . well over the marquee . . . well over the paving stones next to the school building . . .

But what goes up, must come down . . . and down it finally came, heading for the brightly coloured stained-glass window which glinted in the afternoon sunshine above the archway of the rear entrance.

A gasp came from the crowd but, thankfully, at the last moment

almost, the ball seemed to run out of steam and suddenly dropped more steeply. It just missed the window — and struck the huge, ancient clock on the wall below instead.

For one hundred years the clock had peacefully trundled away the passing hours of the school's history, undisturbed. Unlike Sleeping Beauty, however, it wasn't awakened from its century-long slumbers by a gentle kiss, but by a hard cricket ball clonking smack into the middle of its face.

The rusty smaller hand was snapped clean off and clattered on to the paving stones beneath, leaving the big minute hand sagging loosely downwards.

The hypnotic spell was broken, too, and a great cheer went up to greet the Danebridge triumph. Andrew and Chris danced off the pitch together with their arms clumsily locked around each other's shoulders and bats waving up and down. Before long, they were lost to sight in the swarm of excited children, Irene right in the thick of it all.

Mr Jones strolled happily behind them, still shaking his head at what had just happened as Grandad came up alongside him. 'Your Andrew sure *timed* that shot pretty well, didn't he?' the headmaster smiled, attempting a weak joke. 'I've never seen such a big hit.'

'Aye, there was certainly no need for you to signal a six,' Grandad chuckled. 'By the looks of it, that job's being done for you.'

Mr Jones followed his gaze and saw what Grandad meant. The battered old clock was still pointing, with its remaining buckled hand, down at the figure six on the dial, as if in surrender.

THE END